MUSIC FOR ALICE
Allen Say

Houghton Mifflin Company Boston 2004

Walter Lorraine Books

Walter Lorraine *wl* Books

www.houghtonmifflinbooks.com

Library of Congress Cataloging-in-Publication Data

Say, Allen.
  Music for Alice / Allen Say.
      p. cm.
"Walter Lorraine Books."
Summary: A Japanese American farmer recounts her agricultural successes
and setbacks and her enduring love of dance. Based on the true life
story of Alice Sumida, who with her husband Mark established the
largest gladiola bulb farm in the country during the last half of the
twentieth century.
  ISBN 0-618-31118-1
  1. Sumida, Alice—Juvenile fiction. [1. Sumida, Alice—Fiction. 2.
Japanese Americans—Fiction. 3. Agriculture—Fiction. 4. Farms—Fiction.
5. Dance—Fiction.] I. Title.
  PZ7.S2744Mu 2004
  [E]—dc22

                                                        2003014799

Printed in the United States of America
WOZ 10 9 8 7 6 5 4 3 2 1

For Alice Sumida

My name is Alice. I grew up on a farm in California. And ever since I was a little girl I've loved dancing more than anything else. Often I wished Daddy's tractor would turn into a coach and take me dancing, but it only made noise and dust. I went to all the school dances. I loved dancing.

After I finished college I met Mark. He wasn't much of a dancer, but the fox trot isn't hard to learn—you just walk to the music. I married Mark and moved to Seattle, Washington, where he had a business selling seeds to farmers.

It was in our new home that we learned about the bombing of Pearl Harbor by Japanese airplanes. Suddenly the world was at war. A man from the FBI came to search our apartment. Japanese Americans in the area had to report to the assembly center in Portland, Oregon. We had to be ready in two weeks. We could take one suitcase each and nothing more.

"How can our government do this to us?" I asked Mark. He couldn't explain.

The assembly center was an old stockyard. Each family slept in a stall that smelled of cows. We had to stay there until the internment camps were built. It was like a bad dream.

A few days later, a group of white American farmers came looking for volunteers to work on their fields. They said whoever worked for them wouldn't have to go to an internment camp. Some men, who had been farmers, stepped forward. Mark looked at me, and I nodded. We got on the truck with them. I was the only woman.

We were driven to the desert at the eastern edge of Oregon. We were given tents to live in. And early the next morning a caravan of pickup trucks took us out to the field of sugar beets. Our job was to thin the crop, to make spaces between the plants.

"We should have stayed at the assembly center," Mark said.

"We'll be all right," I said, even though I was sorry that we had come.

We watched the other workers and tried to do what they did. In the heat, they wavered like slow dancers. Even the thought of dancing didn't cheer me very much.

When we had finished the job, a government agent came and told us we could go where we liked, as long as we stayed in the county. We were still prisoners, I thought, in a bigger prison. Mark and I looked for a place to live. Luckily a farmer agreed to let us rent an old house.

"We'll fix it up," he said.

"It'll be a palace," I said.

The men we had worked with came and urged us to start a farm. Mark asked the federal agents if we could do this. They said that growing food was so important that the government would loan us the money. We were amazed and delighted. With the loan, we were able to lease two hundred acres of desert land.

The land was full of stones. We had to dig them out of the ground, put them in strong bags, and take them away before we could plant anything. Our first harvest was a harvest of stones.

The sandy soil of the desert gave us a harvest of beautiful smooth-skinned
baking potatoes. We sold some of them to fine Chicago restaurants
and thought we were well on our way to success.

The next season we had a bumper crop of Spanish onions. They were
enormous and sweet, but we could not sell them because the farms
around us had also raised onions. The markets were full of them.

What a strange business, I thought. We were successful farmers,
but we couldn't sell what we raised. We were getting poorer with each
harvest. I worried that we would not be able to pay back the loan.
What was going to happen to us?

While I fretted, Mark read books. Then he and the men plowed the field and planted alfalfa.

"We can't eat alfalfa," I said.

"We are going to feed the land and let it rest," Mark said. I wondered if he was losing his mind.

Then the war ended. It was a time for rejoicing, yet I worried we might still be thought of as enemies. And we didn't have a home to go back to. The farm was our home now.

"We'll be fine," Mark kept telling me. I wasn't sure.

One day a big truck brought us hundreds of big, heavy crates.

When Mark told me what was inside them, I was certain he had lost his mind. He and the men worked day and night. It wasn't long before little shoots came out of the earth. Every day the plants grew taller, looking first like blades and then like swords.

As they grew, they sprouted buds and then bloomed. Two hundred acres of gladioli—sword lilies of pink and white, yellow and purple, apricot and orange. For a moment I forgot about all the hard work in the desert, and even of the war. I wanted to dance through the field. I had almost forgotten that feeling.

But the blossoms lasted only a short while. Mark and the men chopped off the flowers—all of them! Then they dug up the bulbs and buried the flowers.

Mark wrote letters and sent sample bulbs to flower growers all
over the country. Then we waited. It was the hardest year of all, just waiting.
And when our field was again in full bloom, they came. Some
even came in their own airplanes to look at our flowers. They
bought all the bulbs we grew and sent large trucks all the way from
Florida to haul them away.

Often we received more orders than we could fill. It was slow work sorting the bulbs by hand, even with forty people working in two shifts. Mark read more books. He designed a sorting machine. We built warehouses and toolsheds and cottages for the workers and their growing families.

We became the largest gladiola bulb growers in the country, but there was no time for dancing. We worked harder than ever before. The Japanese consul general came from Seattle to marvel at our farm; a famous movie actress traveled all the way from Tokyo to look at our flowers; a Buddhist abbot came from Kyoto to bless us. I was happy, but I kept thinking, What good is success if we can't enjoy ourselves?

Mark asked his nephew to take over the business, but the young man didn't want to live in the desert. In the end we decided to sell the farm.

The day we left, I remembered the time I had gone off to college. I remembered the day Mark and I left our first home in Seattle with our two suitcases. Now we were leaving behind all that we had worked for.

We bought a small farm in California and raised some corn and grapes. Then Mark tried to start a fish farm, to raise colored carp called *koi,* but there wasn't a market for them. During our tenth year at the new place, after a short illness, Mark died. I didn't think about dancing after that.

A few years ago I came to live in Portland, Oregon. It's a place that holds many painful memories, but this is where Mark and I began our journey so long ago, and that makes me feel close to him. My apartment is quite near the old stockyard — the assembly center — but the terrible smells of the place are fading from my mind. Now what I often think of is the field of blooming sword lilies as far as the eye can see.

Last year I went back to the farm. It's hard to believe that I had been away for thirty years. The farm was falling to pieces. Mark would have been sad to see it so. But we had made a small part of the desert bloom with beautiful colors, and now it was returning to what it was before. We had a good life there. As I walked around the place, a wonderful feeling came over me.

"Now I can dance!" I said aloud.

And dance I do—all that I can.